OTTO'S
ORANGE DAY

FRANK CAMMUSO & JAY LYNCH

OTTO'S ORANGE DAY

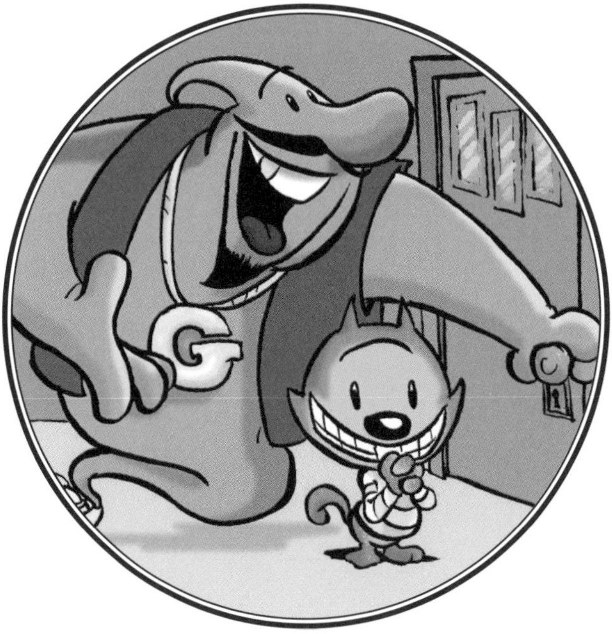
G

A TOON BOOK BY

FRANK CAMMUSO & JAY LYNCH

THE LITTLE LIT LIBRARY, A DIVISION OF RAW JUNIOR, LLC, NEW YORK

Editorial Director: FRANÇOISE MOULY
Advisor: ART SPIEGELMAN

Book Design: FRANÇOISE MOULY & JONATHAN BENNETT

 Library of Congress Control Number: 2007941868

ISBN 13: 978-0-9799238-8-3 ISBN 10: 0-9799238-8-3

Paperback Edition

10 9 8 7 6 5 4 3 2 1

WWW.TOON-BOOKS.COM

For Ngoc

–Frank

For Kathleen and Norah

–Jay

CHAPTER ONE:

MY FAVORITE COLOR!

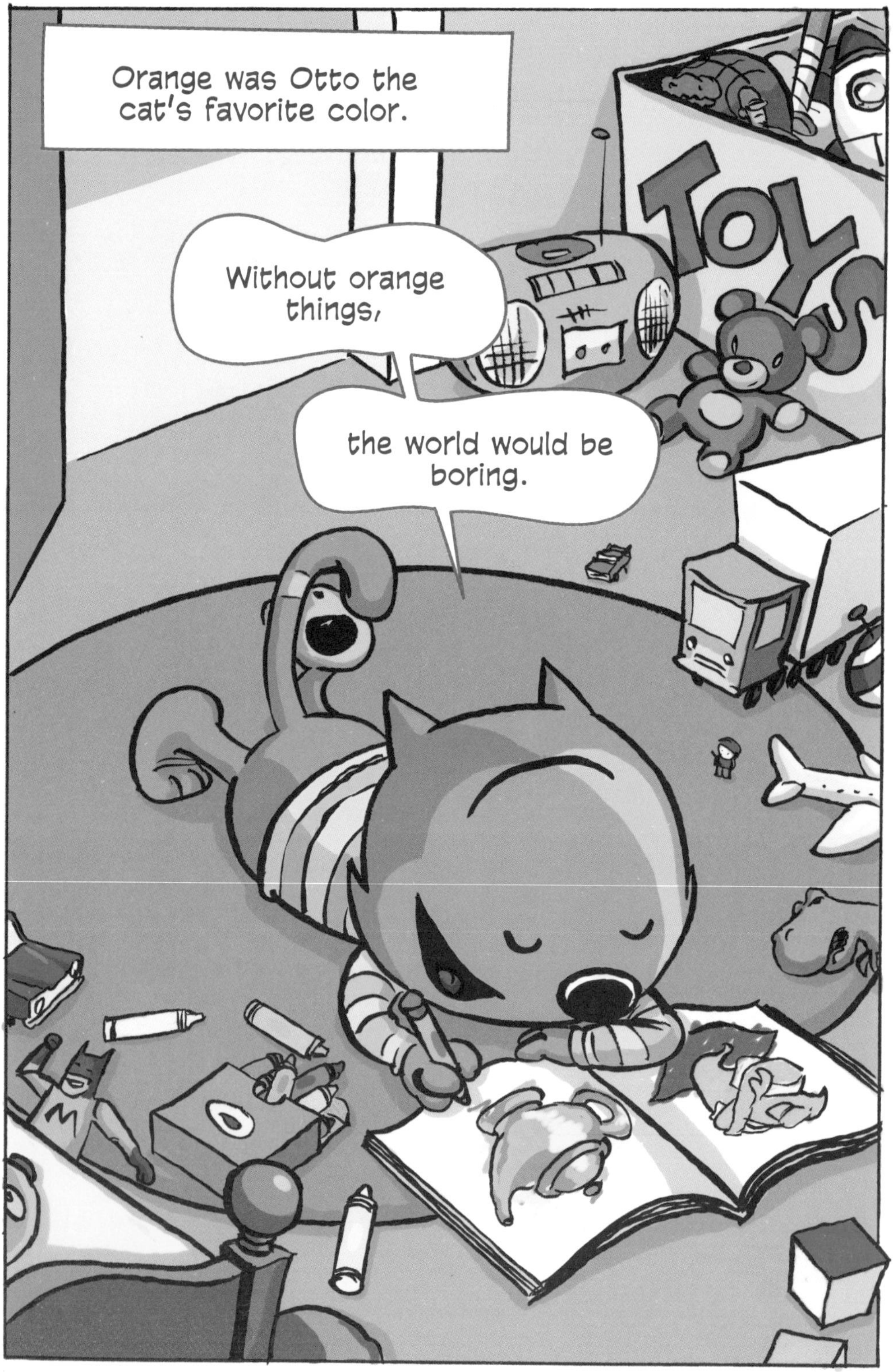
Orange was Otto the cat's favorite color.
Without orange things,
the world would be boring.
TOYS

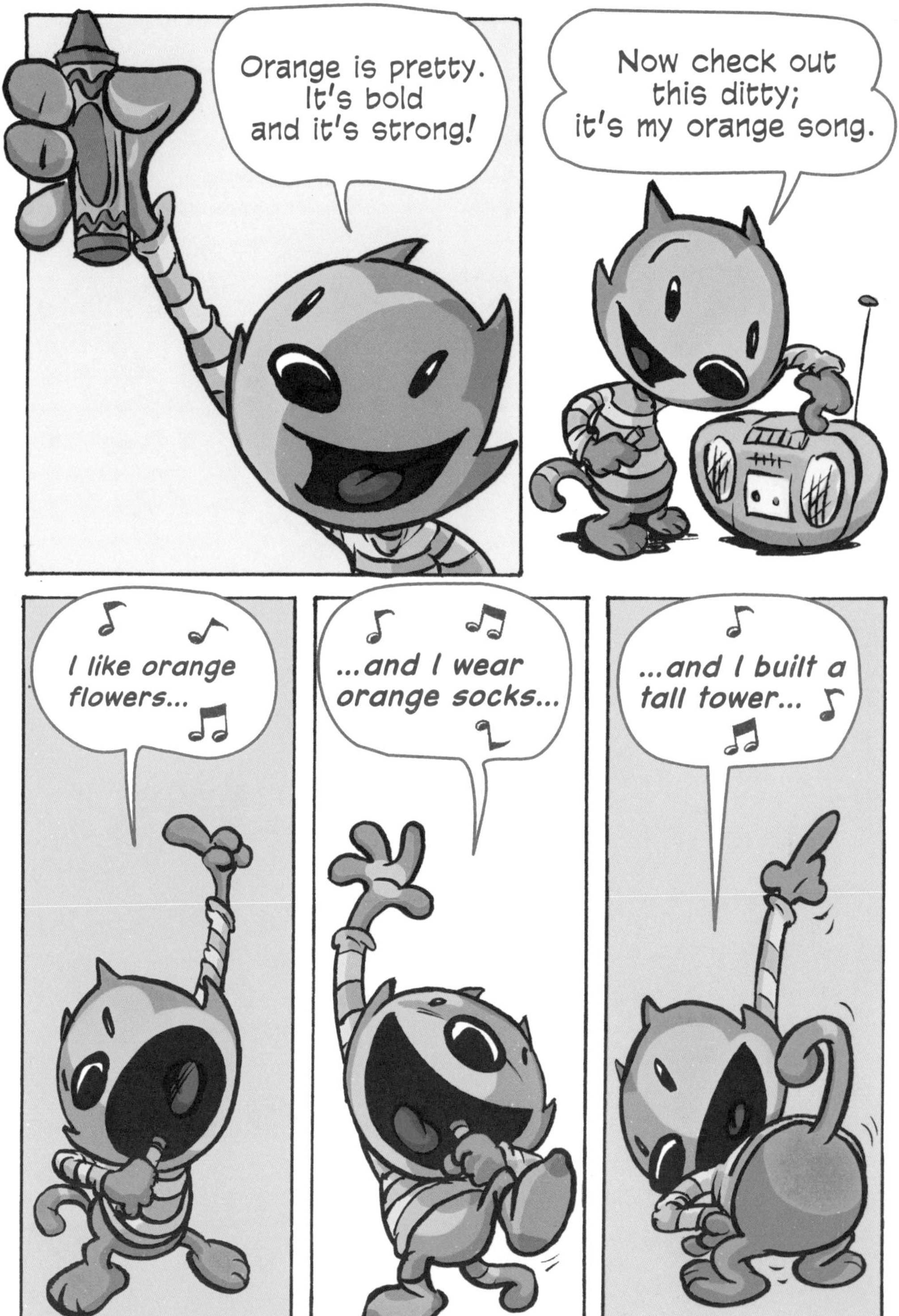
Orange is pretty. It's bold and it's strong!
Now check out this ditty; it's my orange song.
I like orange flowers...
...and I wear orange socks...
...and I built a tall tower...

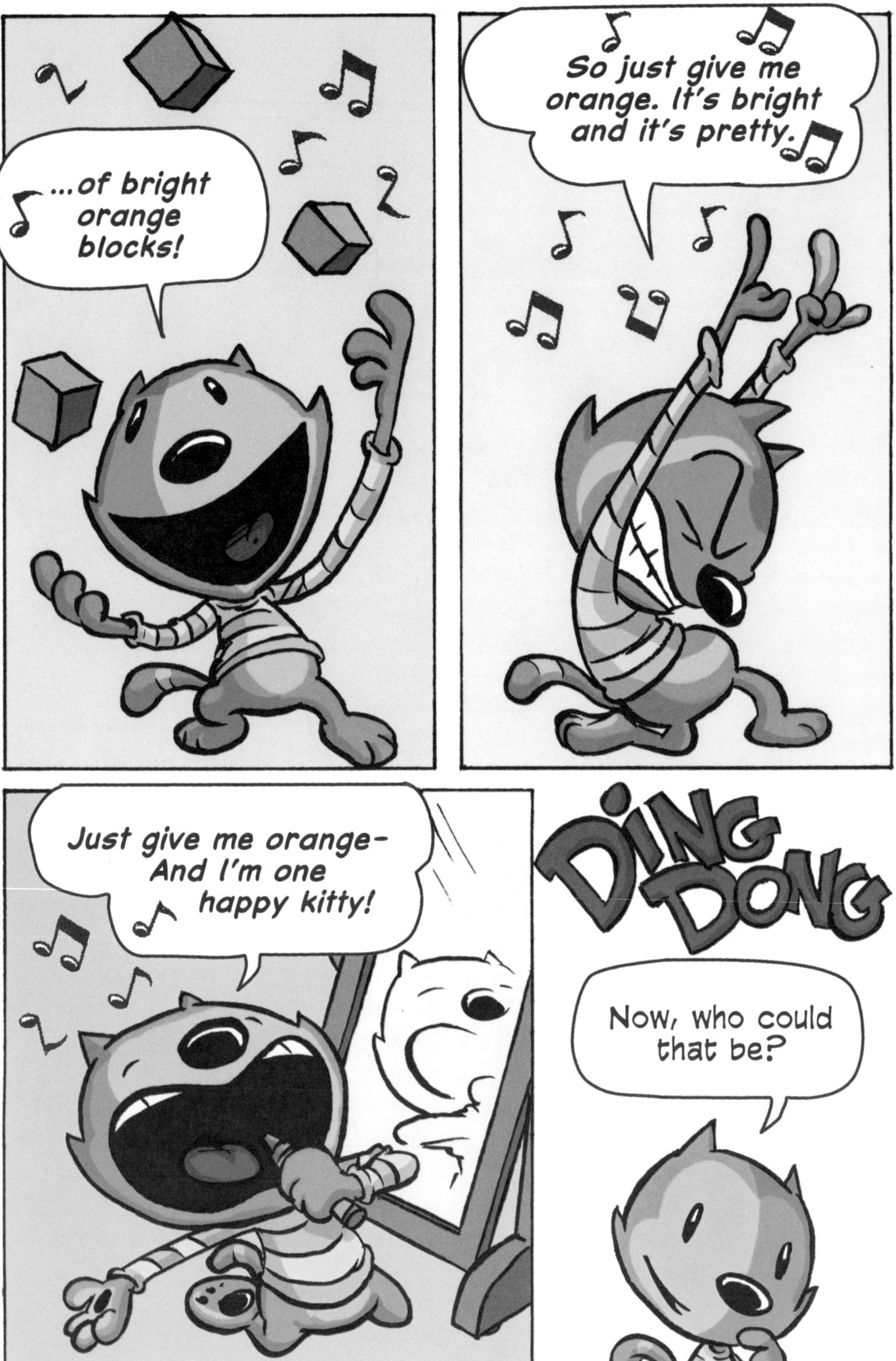
...of bright orange blocks!
So just give me orange. It's bright and it's pretty.
Just give me orange- And I'm one happy kitty!
DING DONG
Now, who could that be?

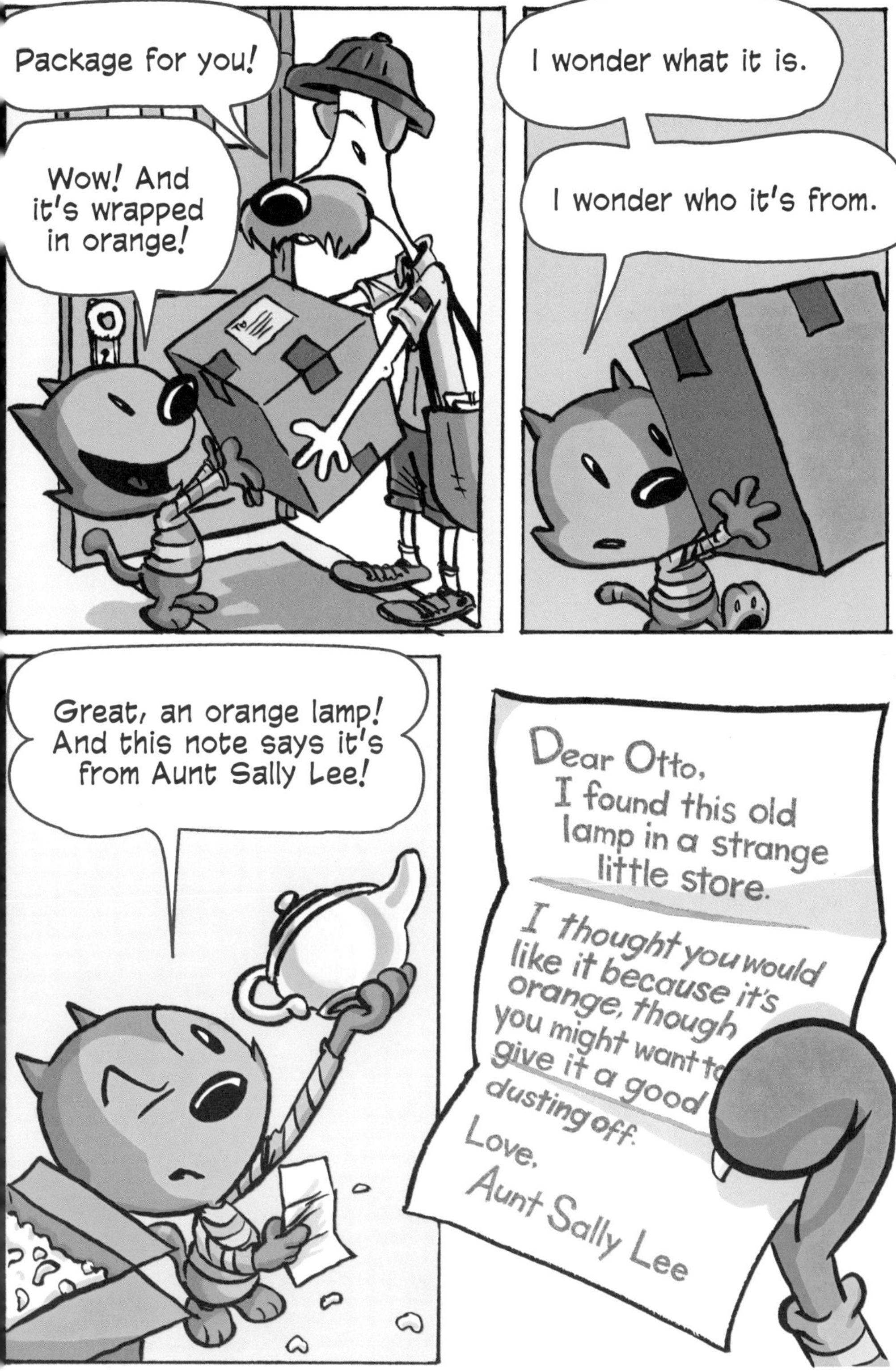
Package for you!
Wow! And it's wrapped in orange!
I wonder what it is.
I wonder who it's from.
Great, an orange lamp! And this note says it's from Aunt Sally Lee!
Dear Otto,
I found this old lamp in a strange little store.
I thought you would like it because it's orange, though you might want to give it a good dusting off.
Love,
Aunt Sally Lee

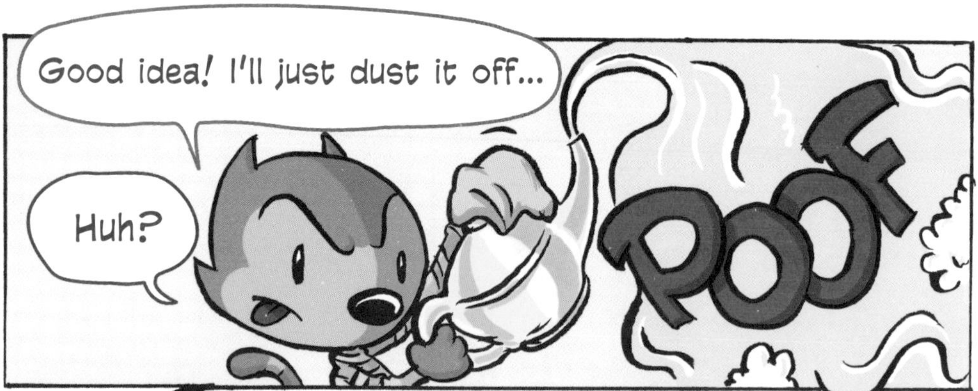
Good idea! I'll just dust it off...
Huh?
POOF

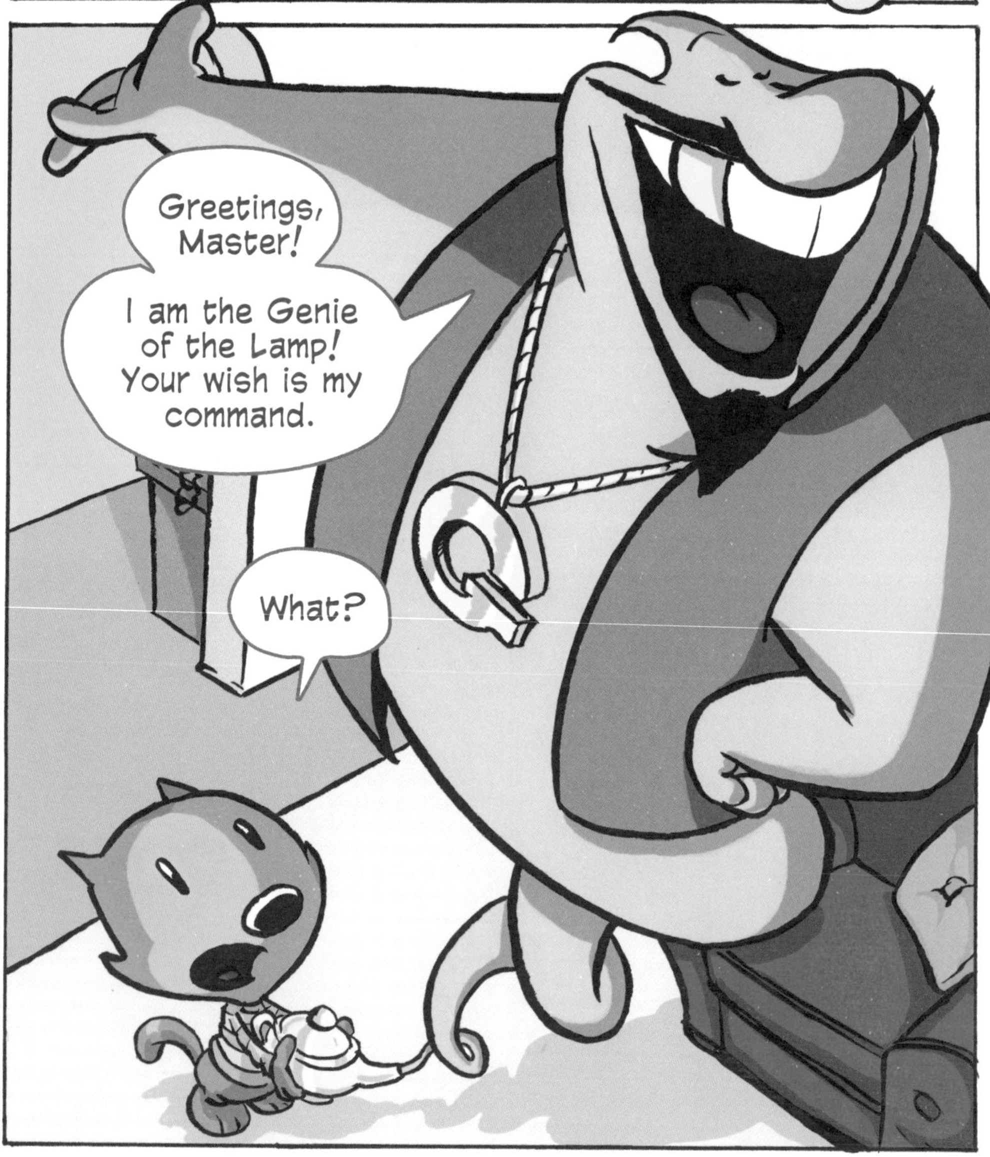
Greetings, Master!
I am the Genie of the Lamp! Your wish is my command.
What?

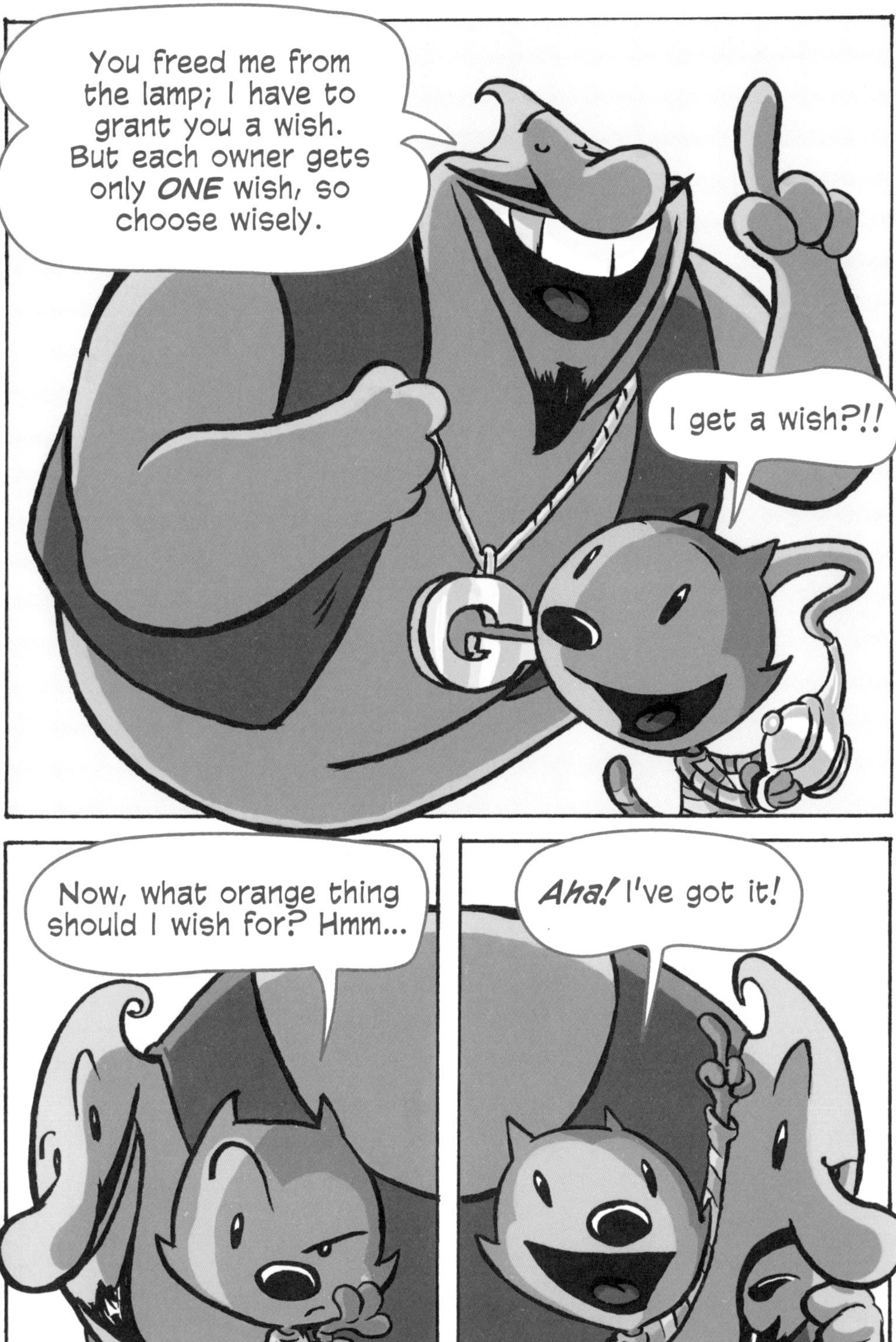
You freed me from the lamp; I have to grant you a wish. But each owner gets only *ONE* wish, so choose wisely.
I get a wish?!!
Now, what orange thing should I wish for? Hmm...
Aha! I've got it!

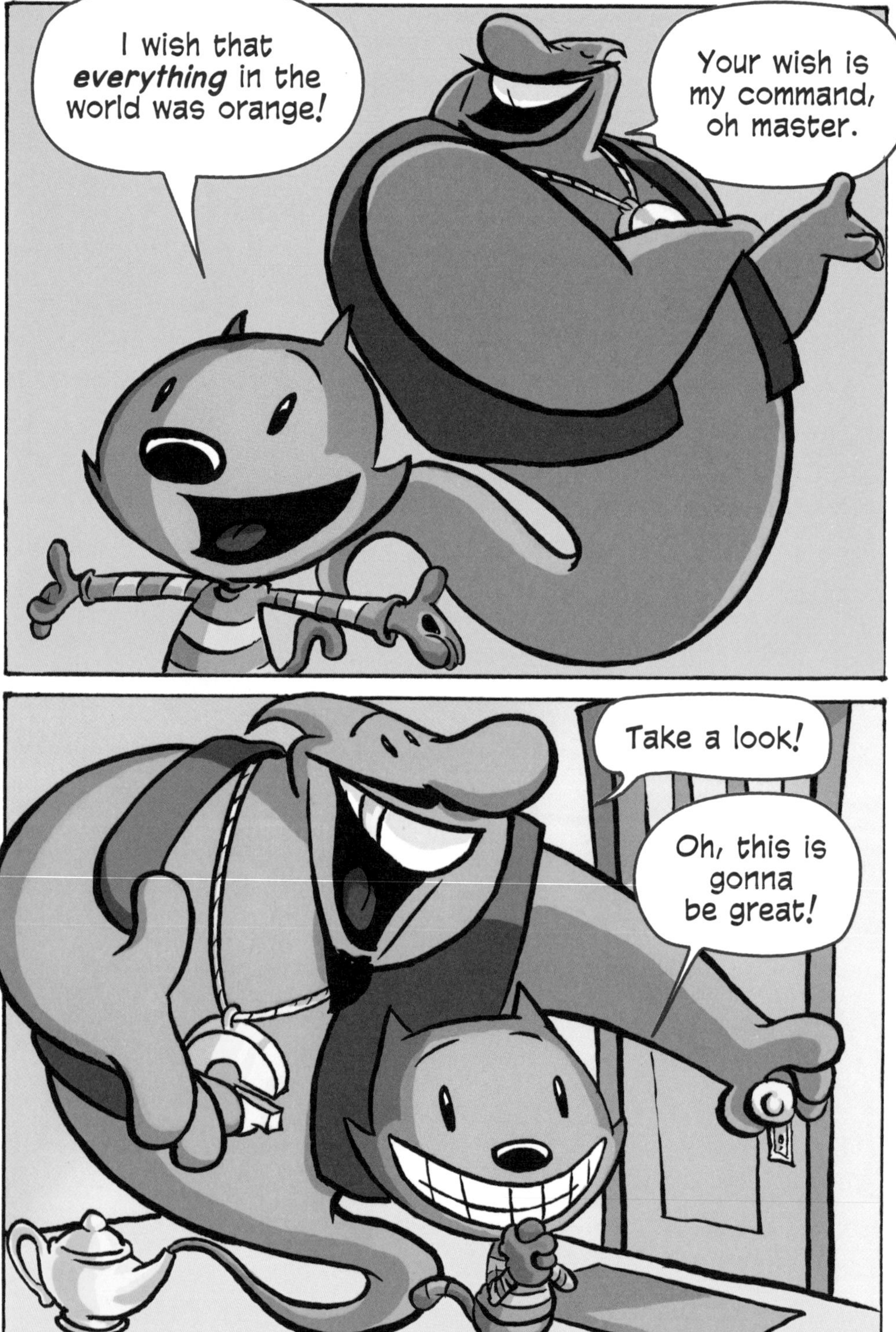
I wish that *everything* in the world was orange!
Your wish is my command, oh master.
Take a look!
Oh, this is gonna be great!

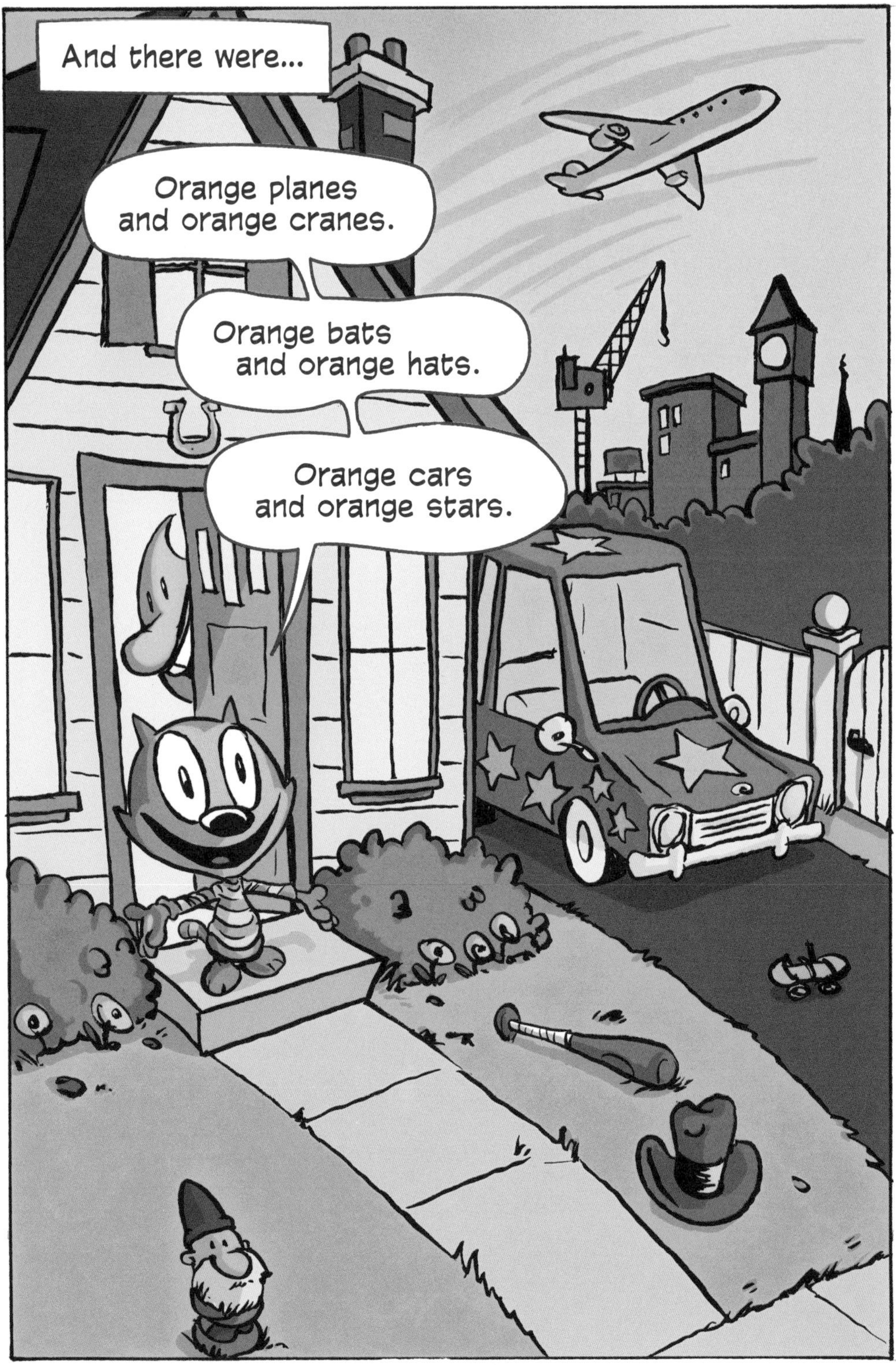
And there were...
Orange planes
and orange cranes.
Orange bats
and orange hats.
Orange cars
and orange stars.

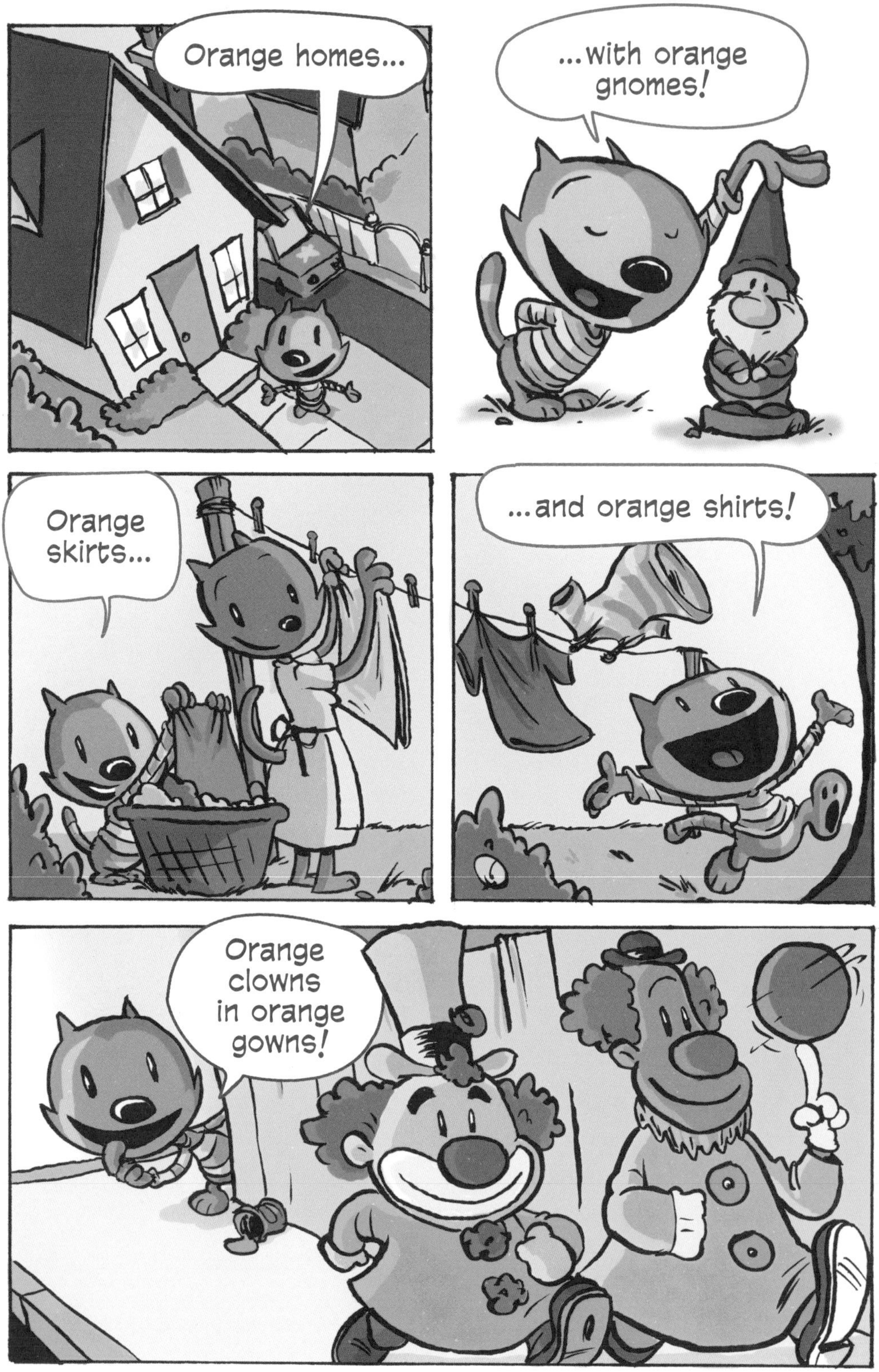
Orange homes...
...with orange gnomes!
Orange skirts...
...and orange shirts!
Orange clowns in orange gowns!

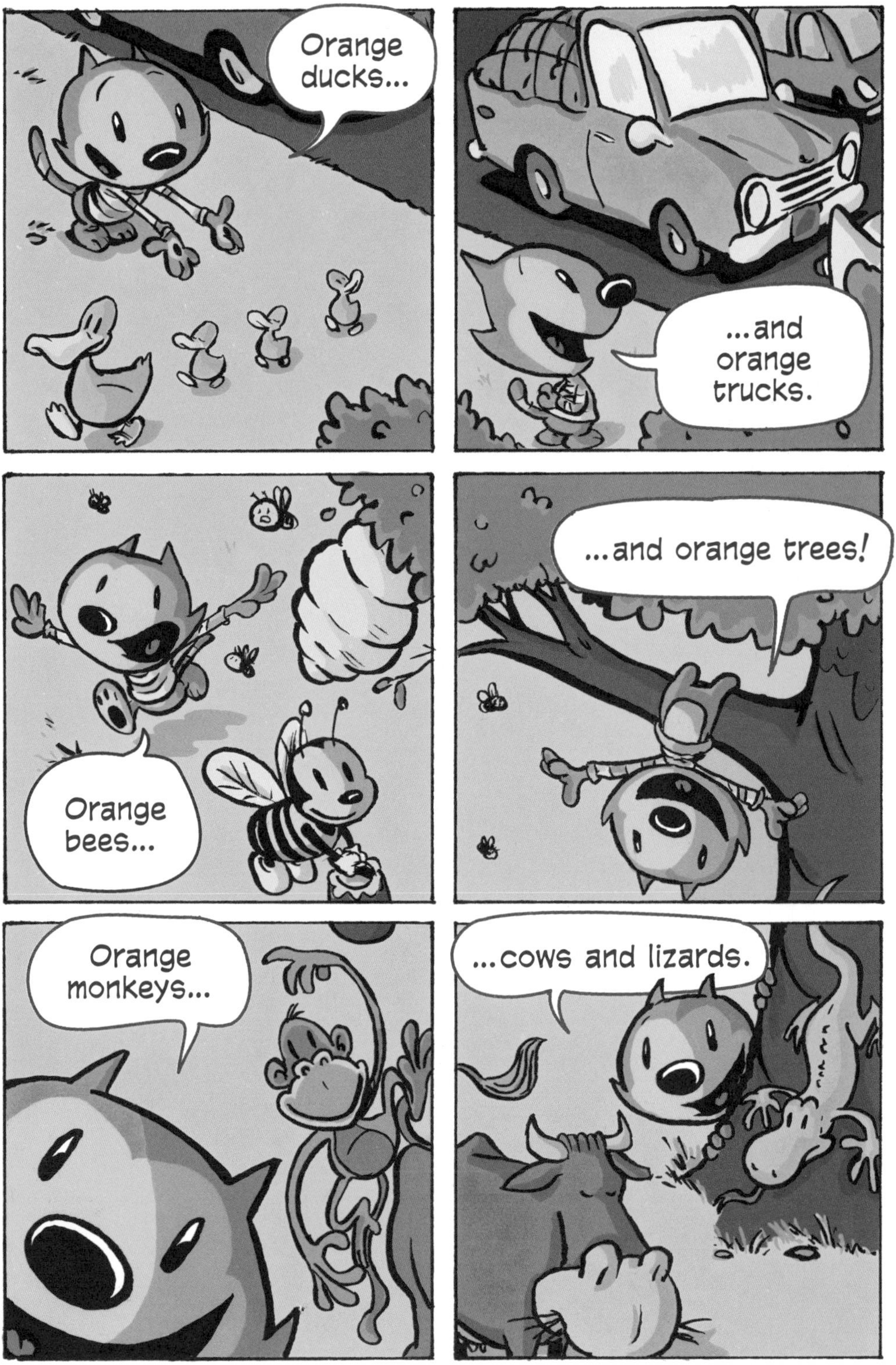
Orange ducks...
...and orange trucks.
Orange bees...
...and orange trees!
Orange monkeys...
...cows and lizards.

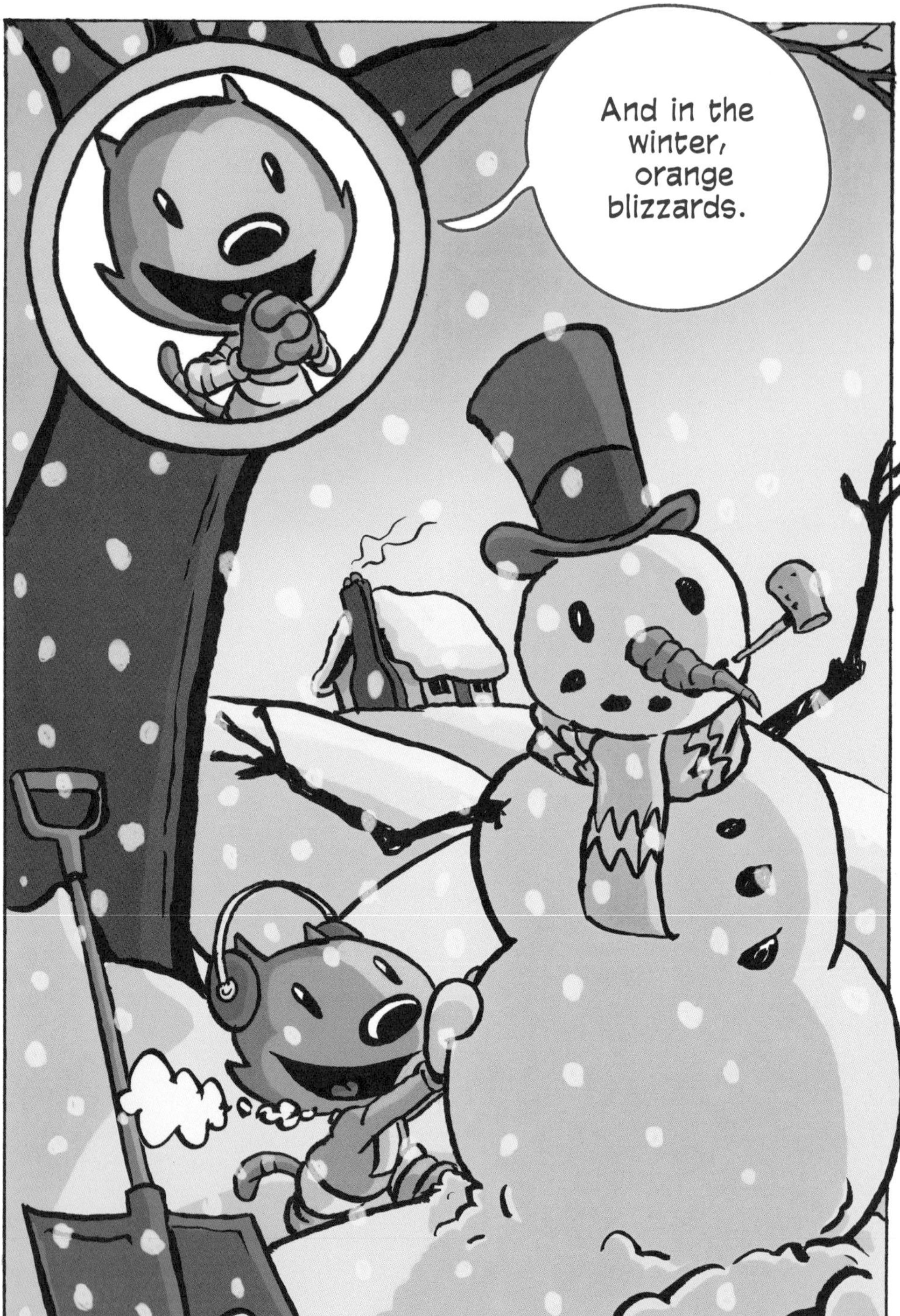
And in the winter, orange blizzards.

CHAPTER TWO:

BE CAREFUL WHAT YOU WISH FOR!

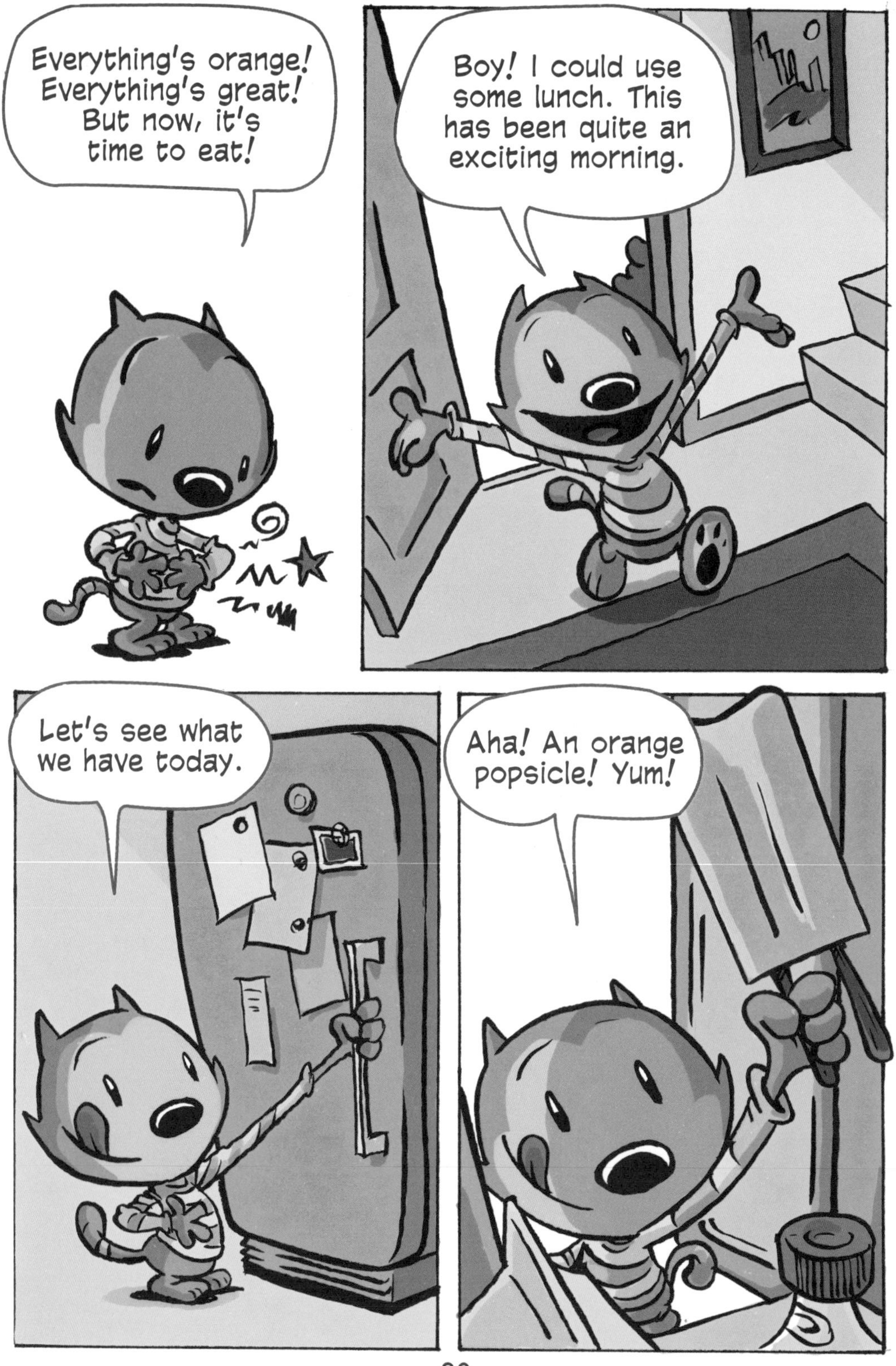
Everything's orange! Everything's great! But now, it's time to eat!
Boy! I could use some lunch. This has been quite an exciting morning.
Let's see what we have today.
Aha! An orange popsicle! Yum!

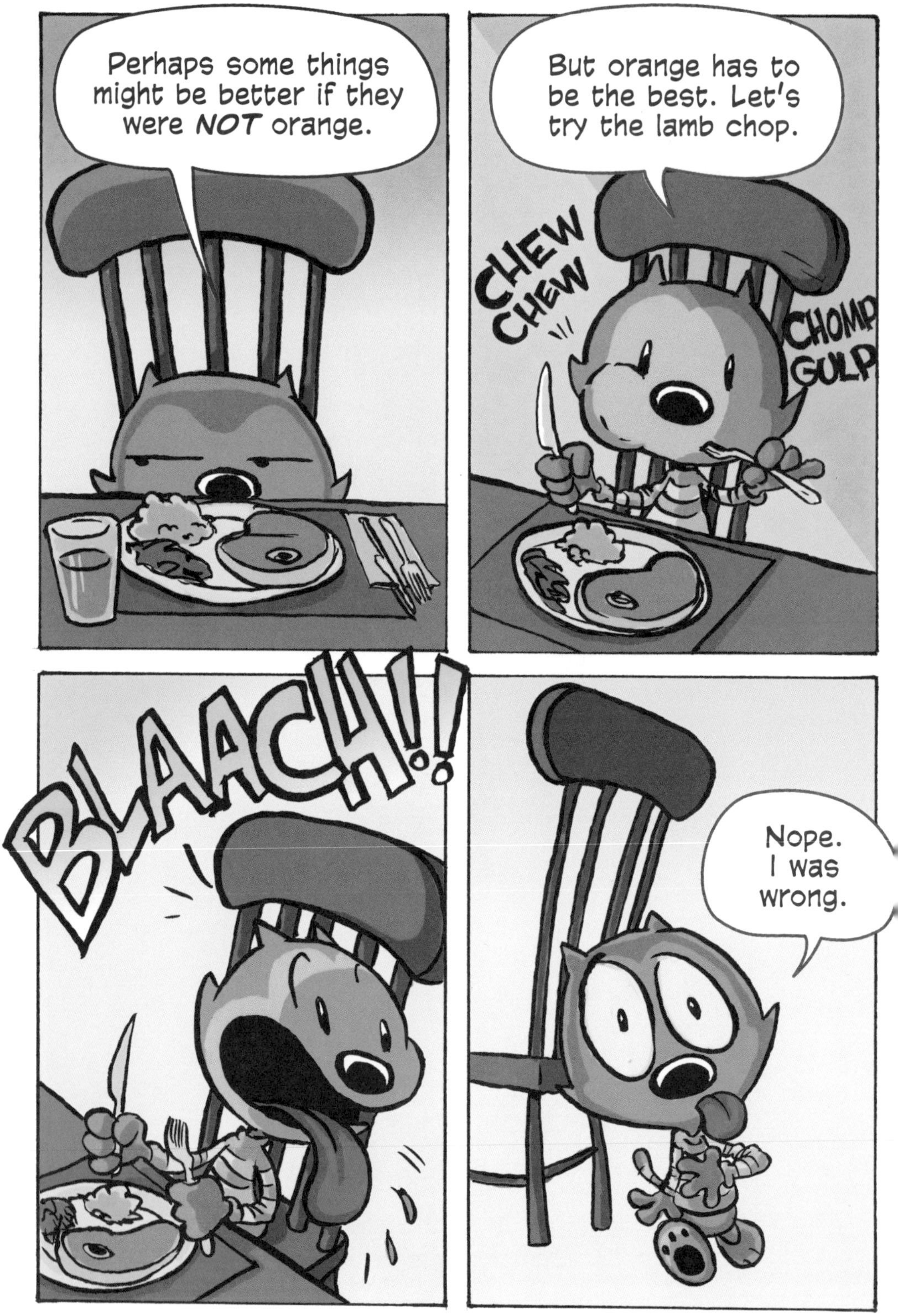
Perhaps some things might be better if they were *NOT* orange.
But orange has to be the best. Let's try the lamb chop.
CHEW CHEW
CHOMP GULP
BLAACH!!
Nope. I was wrong.

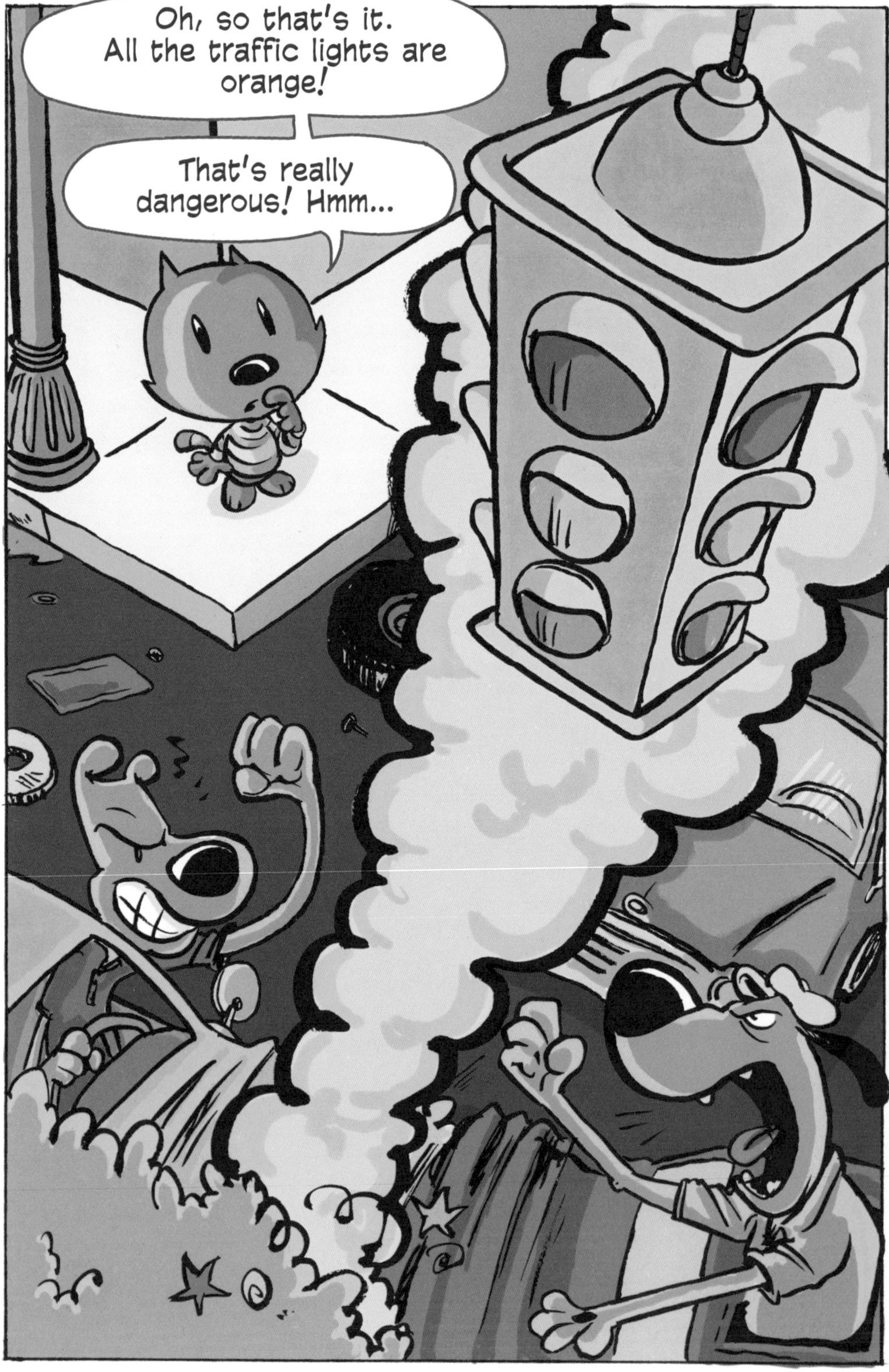
Oh, so that's it. All the traffic lights are orange!
That's really dangerous! Hmm...

25

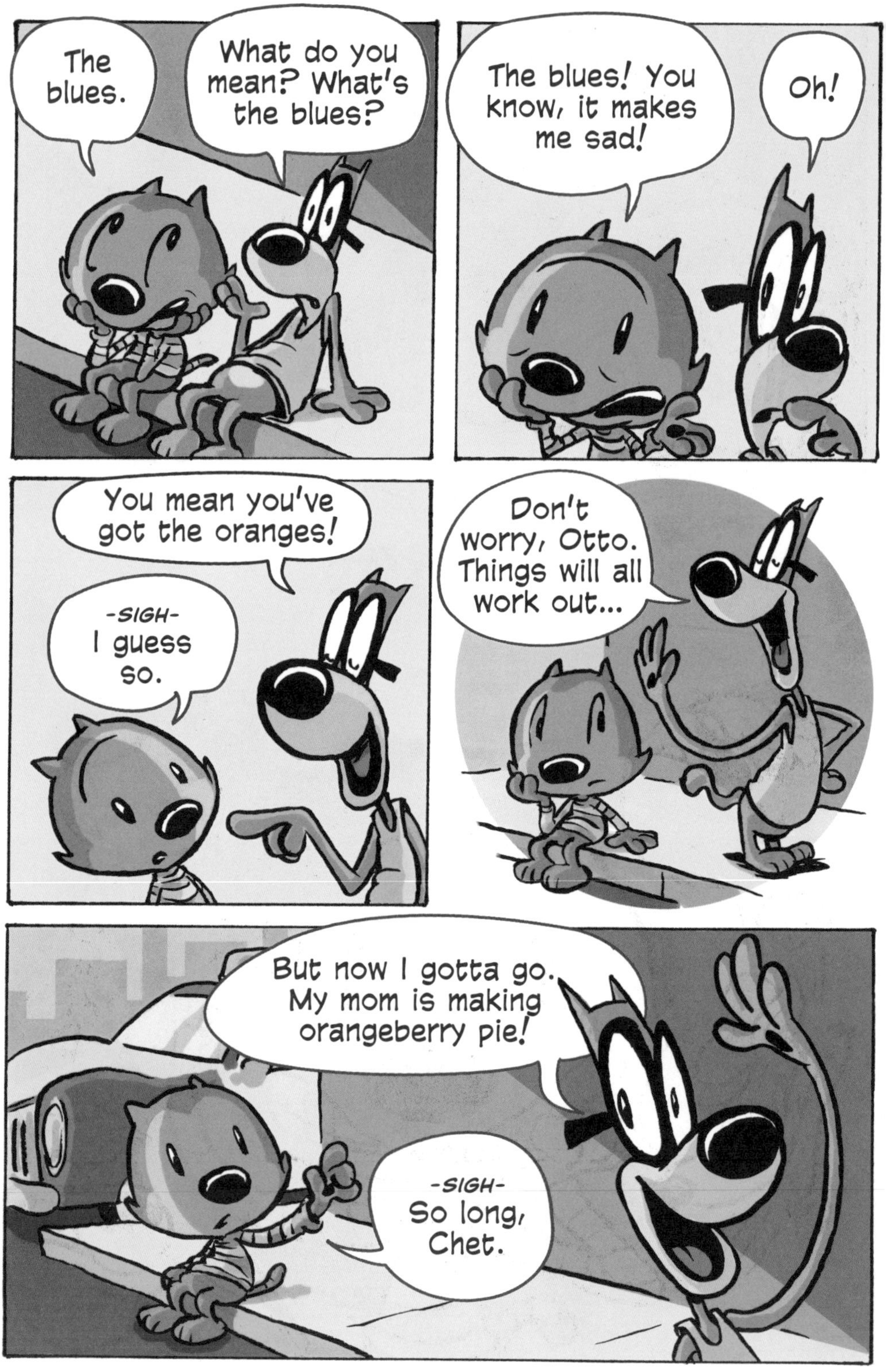
The blues.
What do you mean? What's the blues?
The blues! You know, it makes me sad!
Oh!
You mean you've got the oranges!
-SIGH- I guess so.
Don't worry, Otto. Things will all work out...
But now I gotta go. My mom is making orangeberry pie!
-SIGH- So long, Chet.

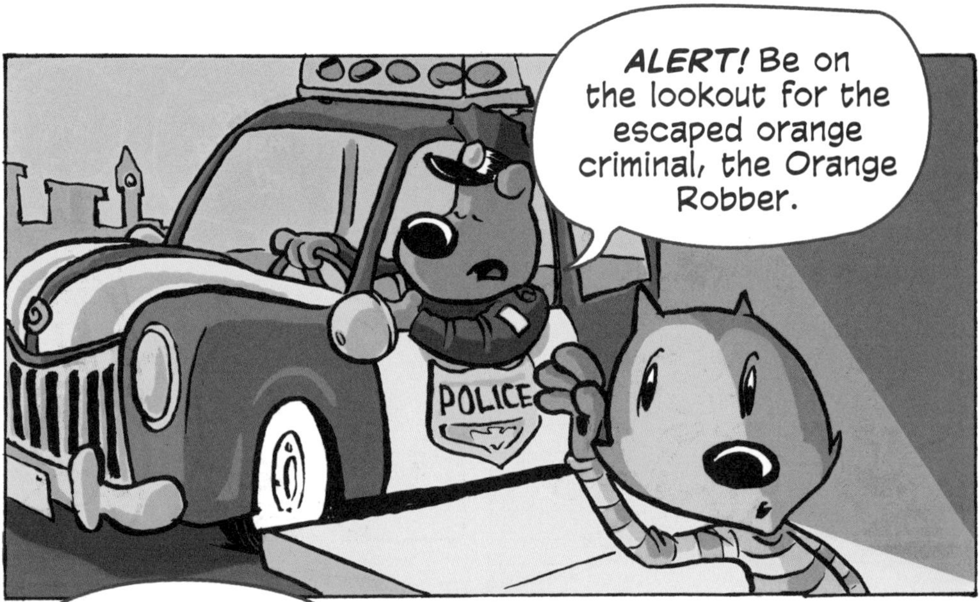
ALERT! Be on the lookout for the escaped orange criminal, the Orange Robber.
POLICE

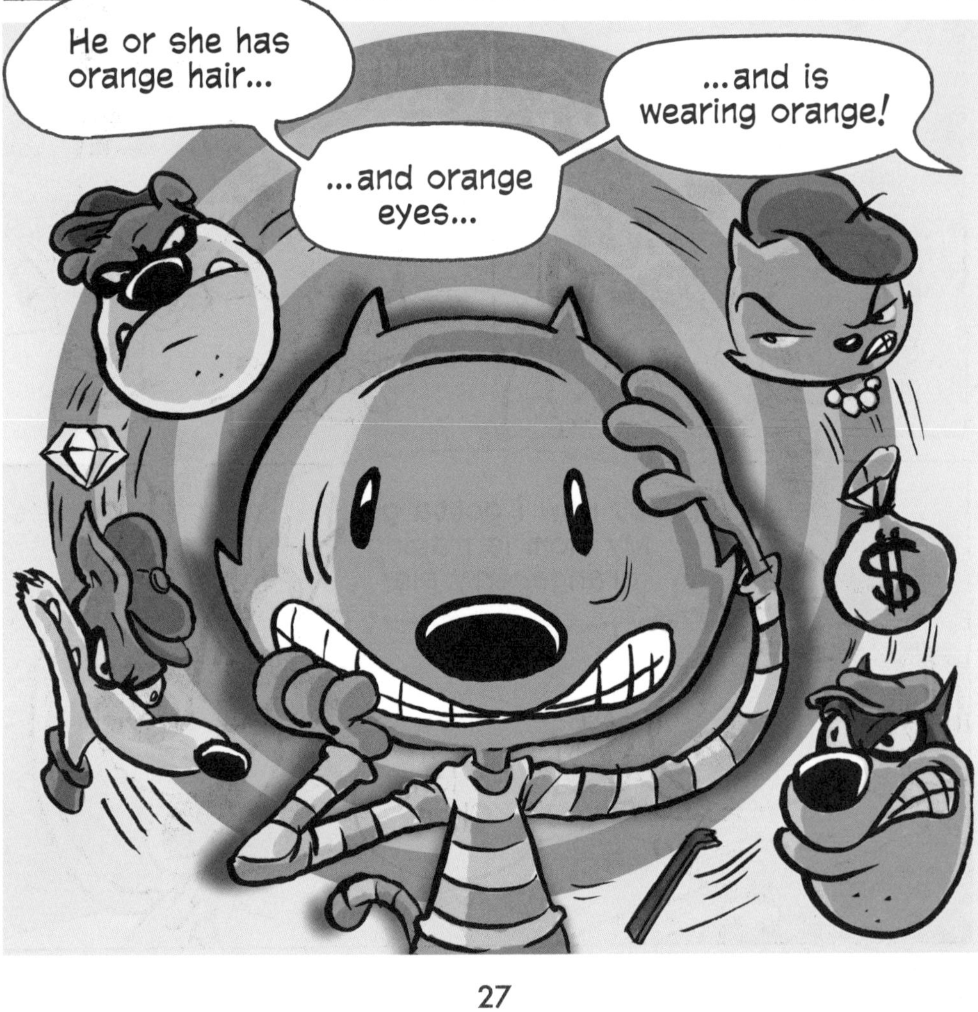
He or she has orange hair...
...and orange eyes...
...and is wearing orange!
$

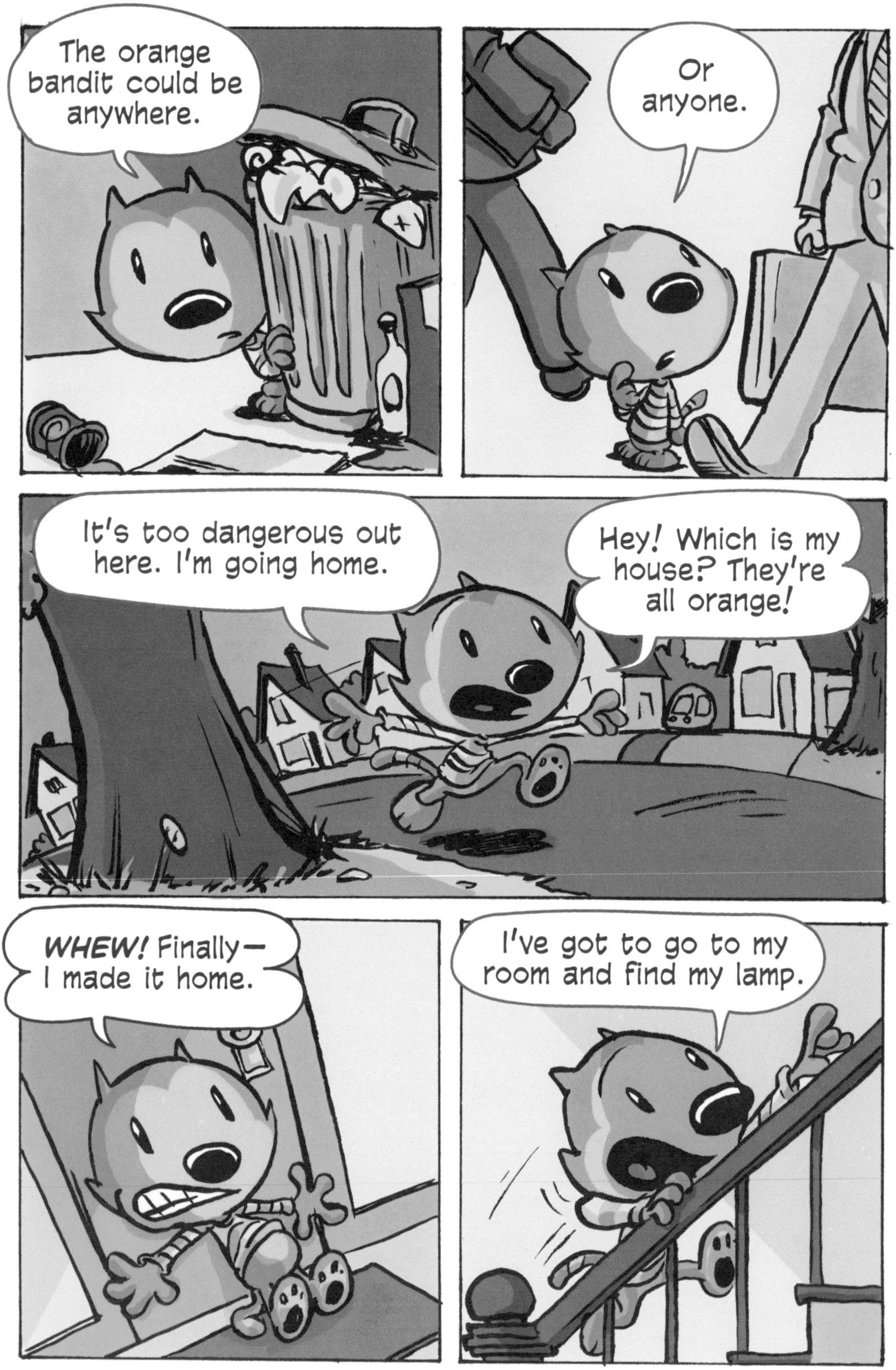
The orange bandit could be anywhere.
Or anyone.
It's too dangerous out here. I'm going home.
Hey! Which is my house? They're all orange!
WHEW! Finally— I made it home.
I've got to go to my room and find my lamp.

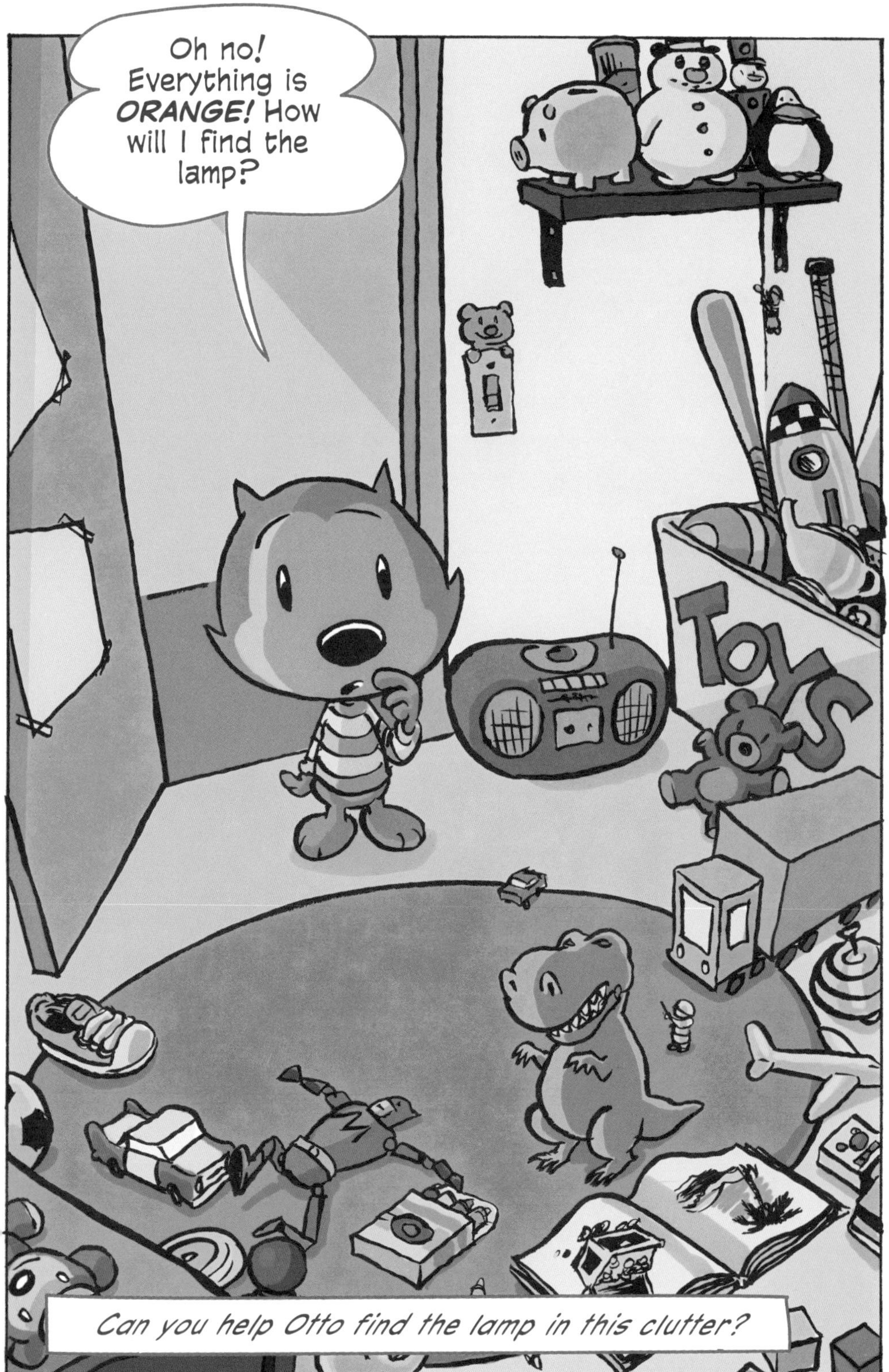
Oh no! Everything is ORANGE! How will I find the lamp?
TOYS
Can you help Otto find the lamp in this clutter?

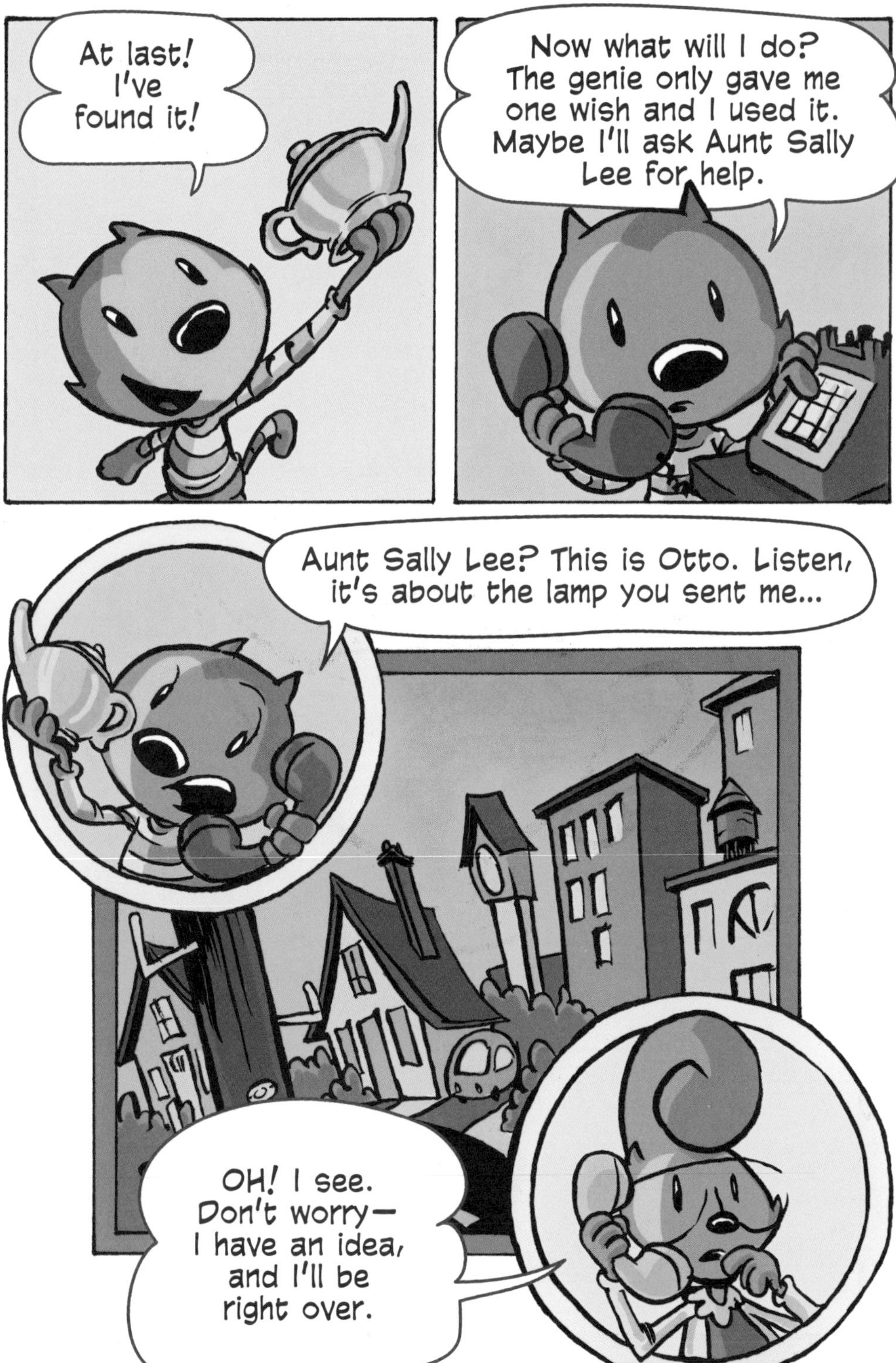
At last! I've found it!
Now what will I do? The genie only gave me one wish and I used it. Maybe I'll ask Aunt Sally Lee for help.
Aunt Sally Lee? This is Otto. Listen, it's about the lamp you sent me...
OH! I see. Don't worry— I have an idea, and I'll be right over.

CHAPTER THREE:

A NEW WISH

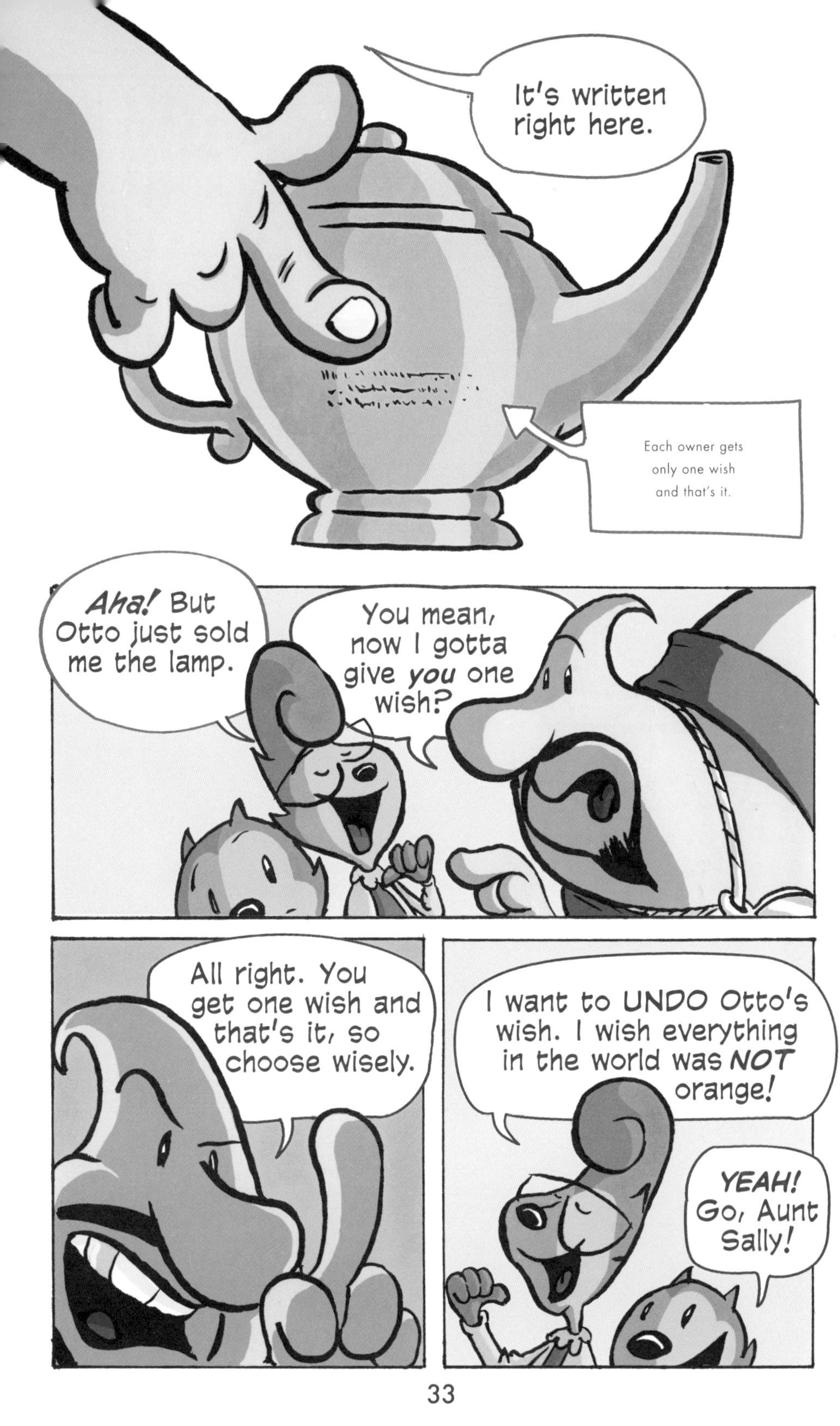
It's written right here.
Each owner gets only one wish and that's it.
Aha! But Otto just sold me the lamp.
You mean, now I gotta give you one wish?
All right. You get one wish and that's it, so choose wisely.
I want to UNDO Otto's wish. I wish everything in the world was NOT orange!
YEAH! Go, Aunt Sally!

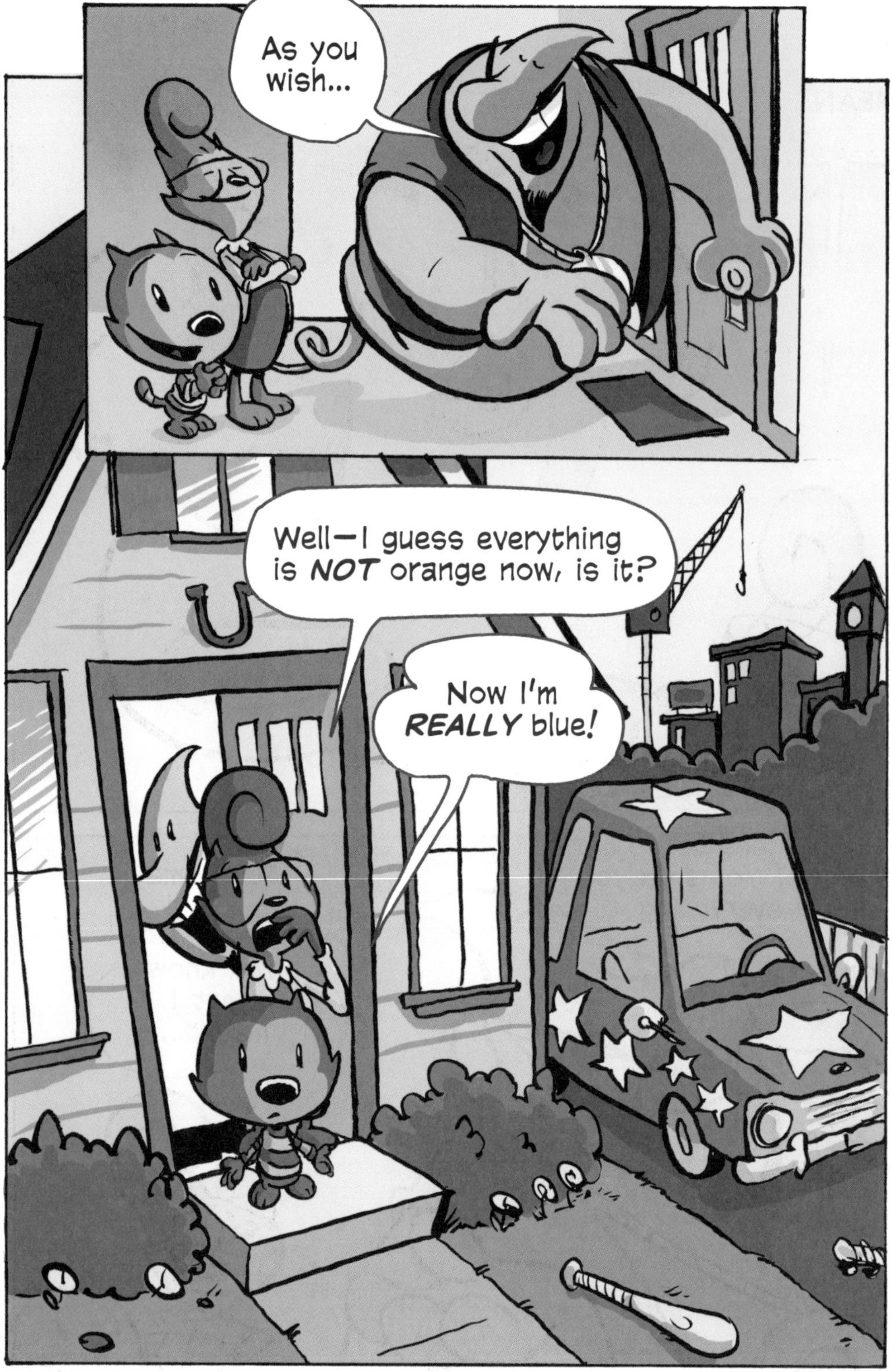
As you wish...
Well—I guess everything is NOT orange now, is it?
Now I'm REALLY blue!

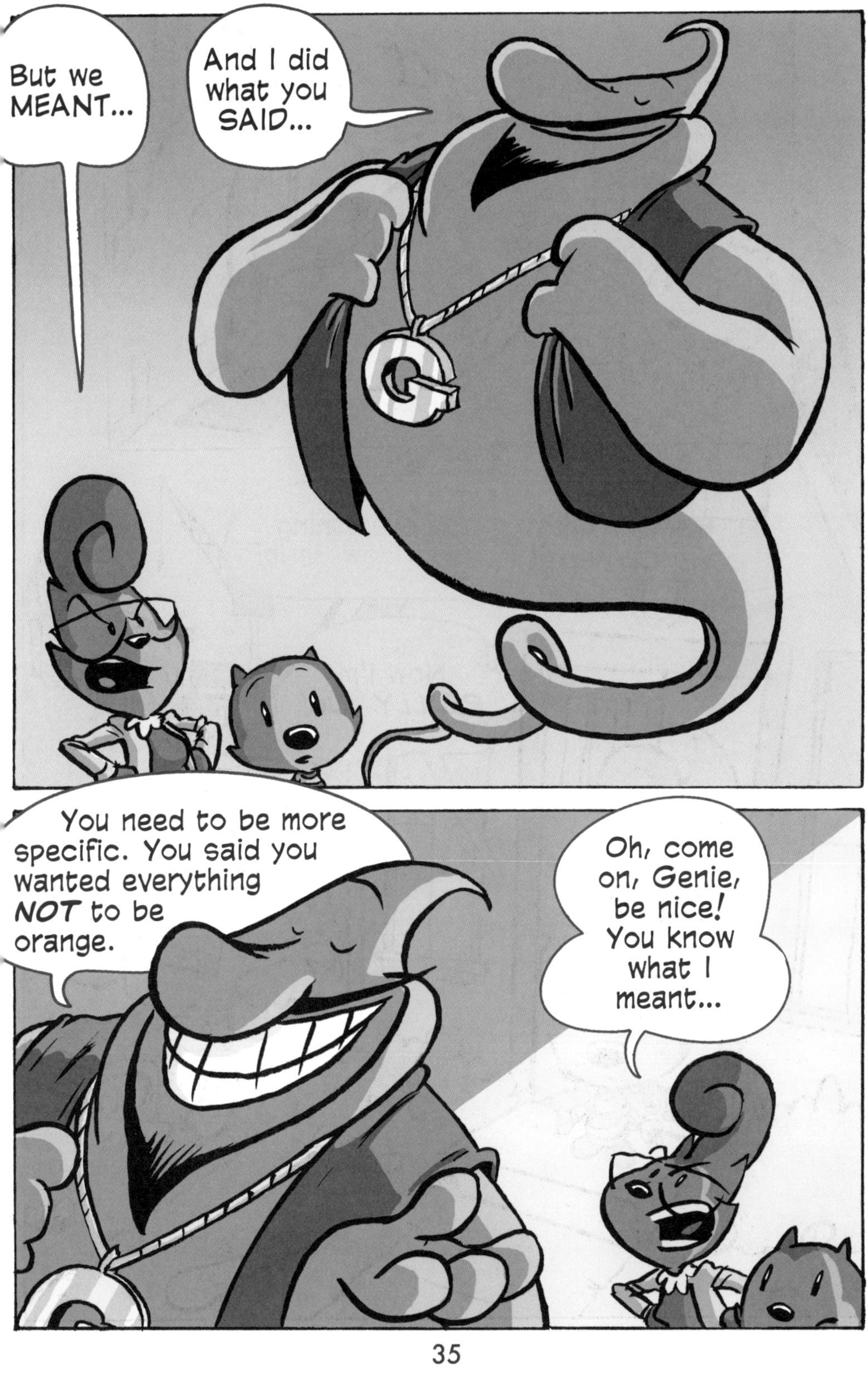
But we MEANT...
And I did what you SAID...
You need to be more specific. You said you wanted everything NOT to be orange.
Oh, come on, Genie, be nice! You know what I meant...

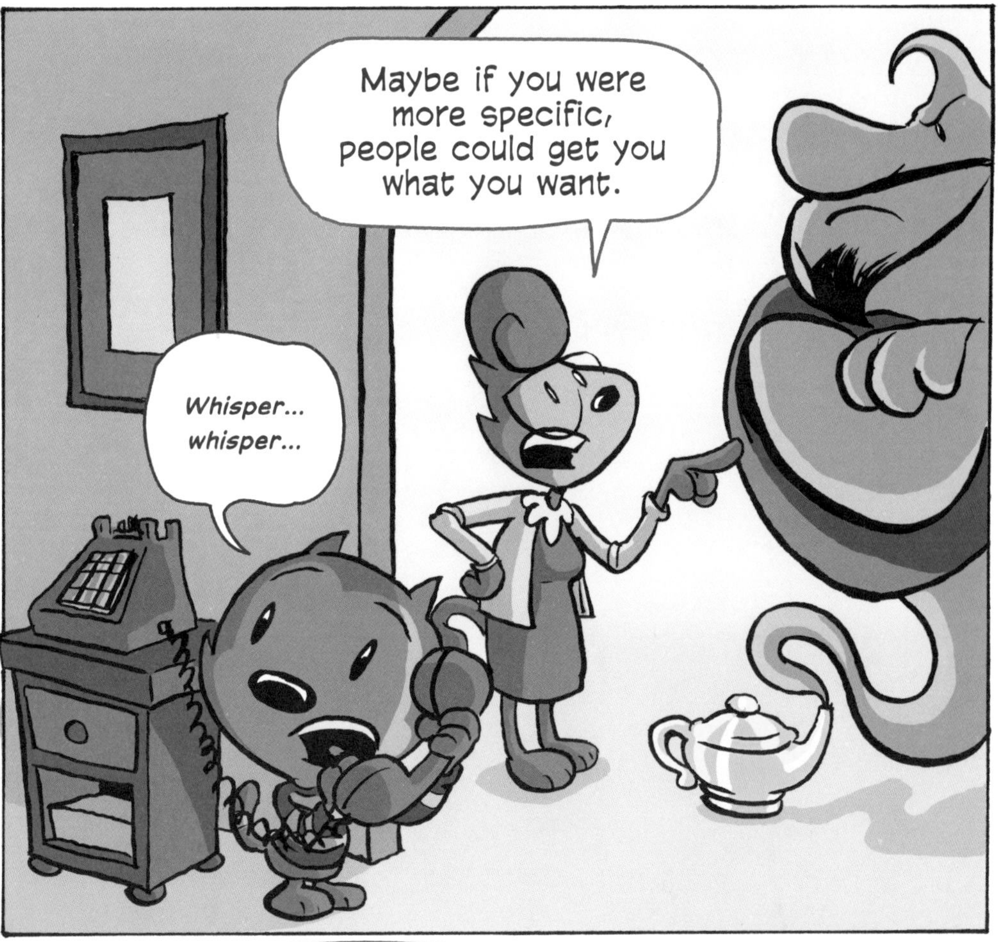
Maybe if you were more specific, people could get you what you want.
Whisper... whisper...

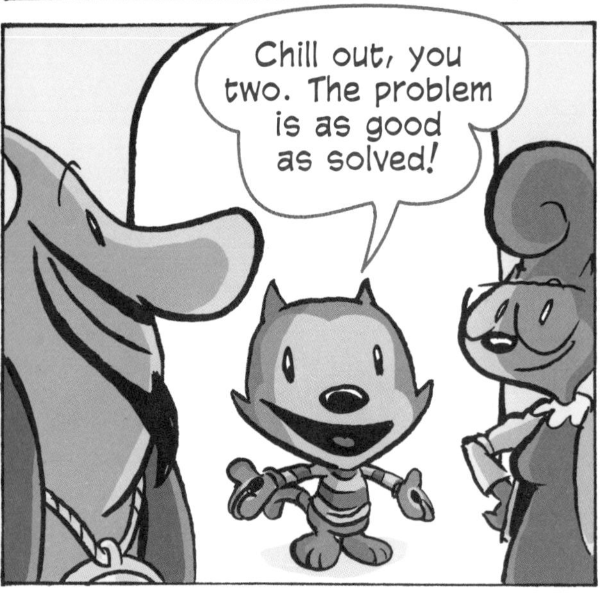
Chill out, you two. The problem is as good as solved!

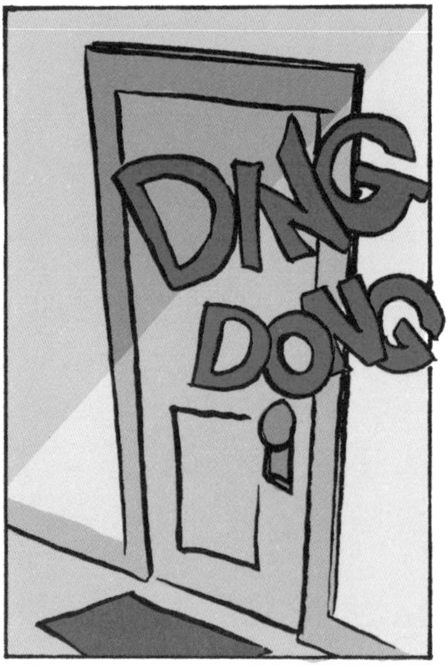
DING DONG

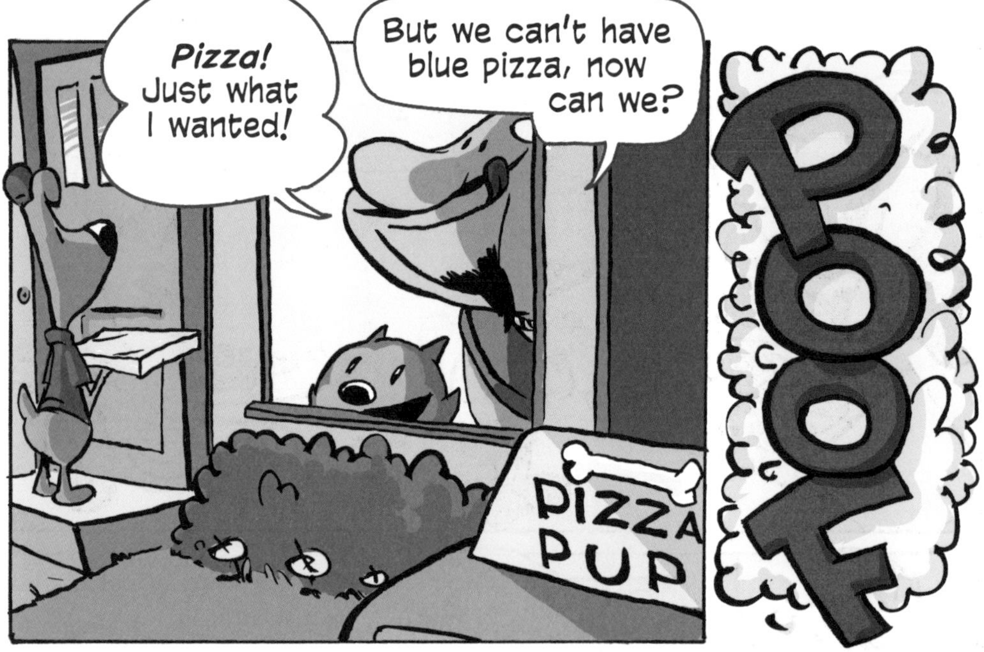
Pizza! Just what I wanted!
But we can't have blue pizza, now can we?
PIZZA PUP
POOF

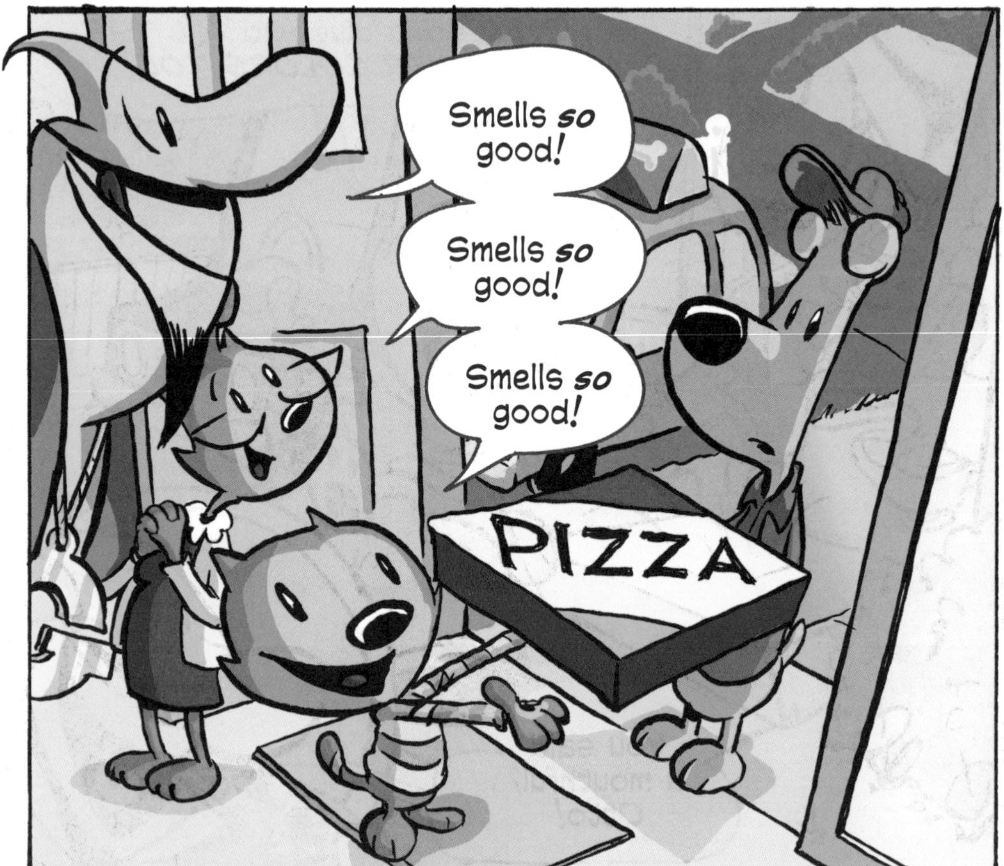
Smells *so* good!
Smells *so* good!
Smells *so* good!
PIZZA

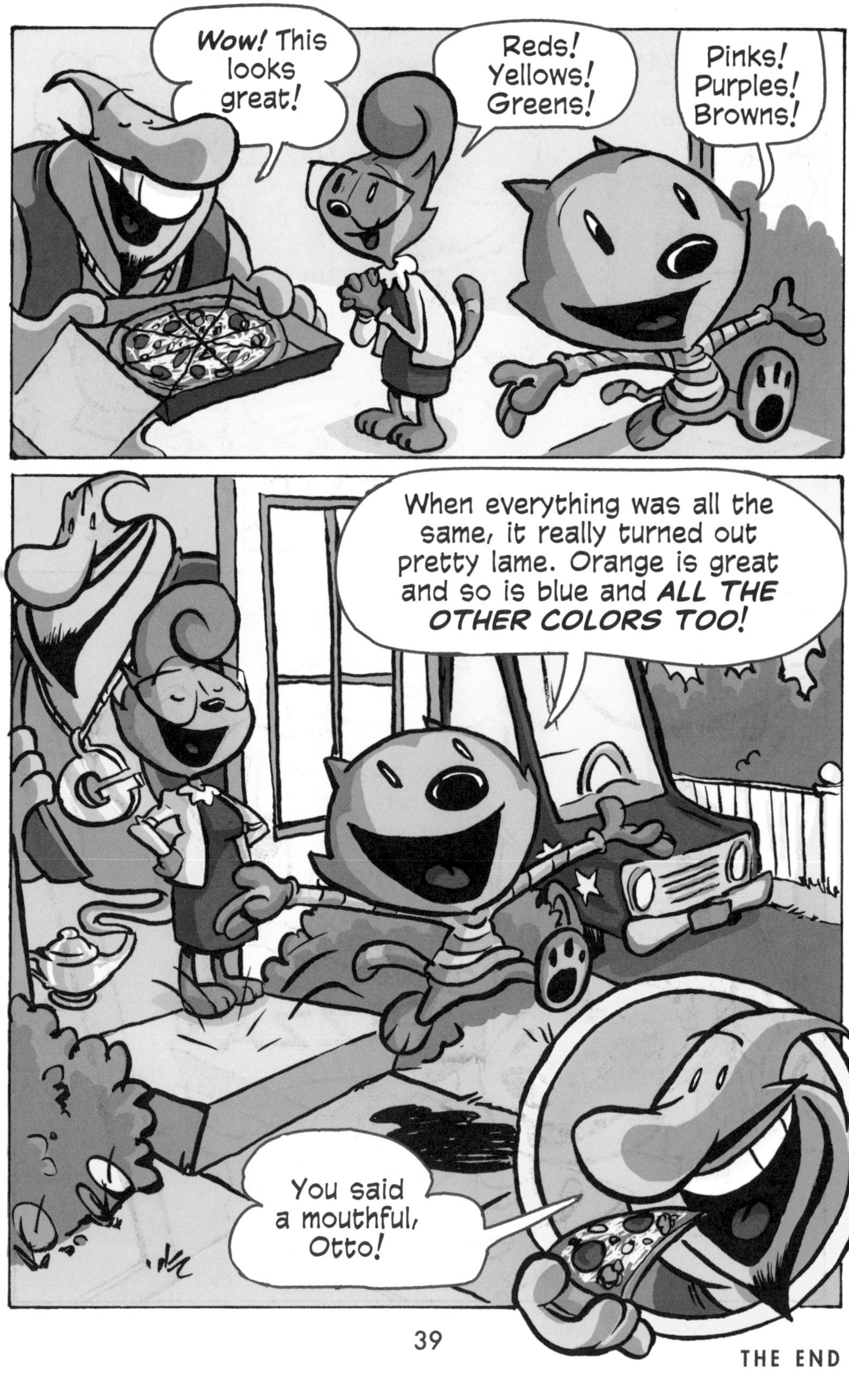
Wow! This looks great!
Reds! Yellows! Greens!
Pinks! Purples! Browns!
When everything was all the same, it really turned out pretty lame. Orange is great and so is blue and ***ALL THE OTHER COLORS TOO!***
You said a mouthful, Otto!

THE END

ABOUT THE AUTHORS

JAY LYNCH, who wrote Otto's story, was born in Orange, NJ, (honest, ORANGE, NJ!) and now lives in upstate New York with his wife, his dog, and way too many cats. He is the founder of *Bijou Funnies,* one of the first and most important underground comics of the Sixties, and for many years wrote the weekly syndicated comic strip, *Phoebe and the Pigeon People.* He has helped create some of Topps Chewing Gum's most popular humor products, such as *Wacky Packages* and *Garbage Pail Kids.*

FRANK CAMMUSO, who drew Otto's adventure, lives in Syracuse, New York, where he is the award-winning political cartoonist for the *Syracuse Post-Standard.* He is the Eisner-nominated creator of *Max Hamm Fairy Tale Detective,* selected as one of the Top Ten Graphic Novels of 2006 by Booklist, and is at work on *Knights of the Lunch Table,* a middle school version of King Arthur and his Knights. His writing has appeared in *The New Yorker, The New York Times, The Village Voice* and *Slate.*